Rhode Island College Junior Class

The Grist

Rhode Island College Junior Class

The Grist

ISBN/EAN: 9783741172519

Manufactured in Europe, USA, Canada, Australia, Japa

Cover: Foto ©Andreas Hilbeck / pixelio.de

Manufactured and distributed by brebook publishing software
(www.brebook.com)

Rhode Island College Junior Class

The Grist

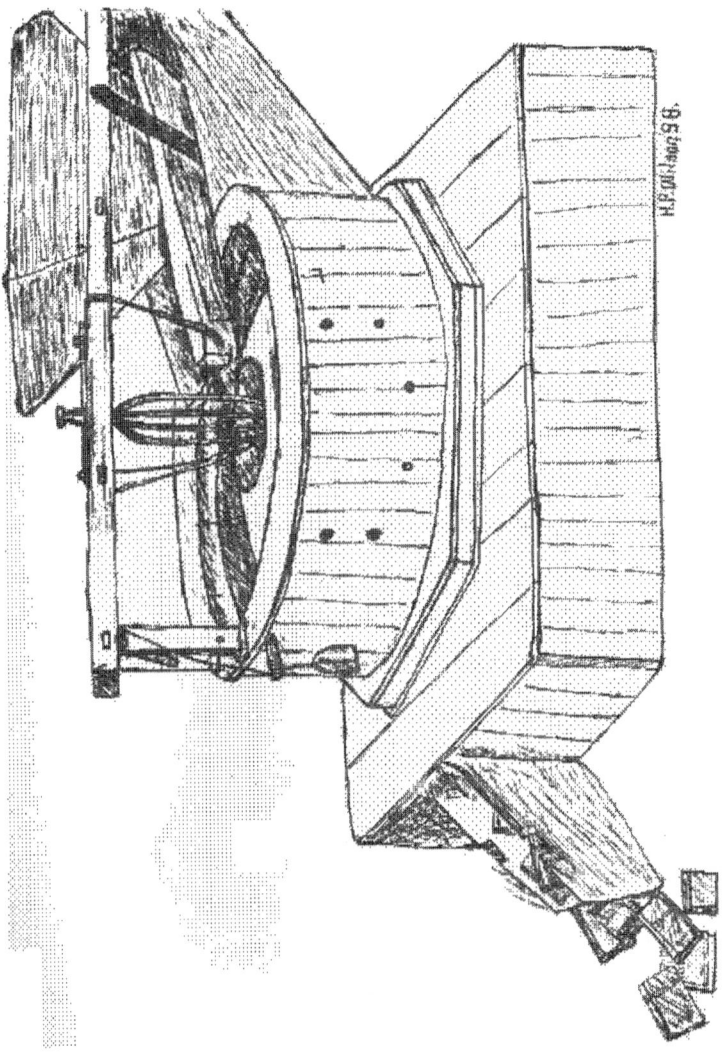

The Grist.

Published by the Junior Class
of the
Rhode Island College
of
Agriculture and Mechanic Arts.

Volume 1.

Kingston, Rhode Island,

June, 1897.

Contents.

Dedication.

TO

Miss Bosworth,

OUR PRECEPTRESS AND CLASSMATE,

WE,

WHO HONOR HER ABILITY AND VALUE HER FRIENDSHIP,

RESPECTFULLY DEDICATE

THIS VOLUME.

Introduction.

———

IN presenting this work to you we would not have
you deceived by its contents. If you would pore
over scientific facts and investigations, or trace the
courses of nations and their great peoples, waste not
your time in searching these pages. But if, on the
contrary, you desire a knowledge of the College, the
student-body, or a few characteristic or humorous epi-
sodes, then perhaps you may find within that for which
you seek.

Since '98 is the first to attempt the publication of
an Annual, we have been without precedent as to what
to publish and what to omit. This has been in some
ways an advantage and in many a disadvantage, par-
ticularly the latter as regards the time allowed us to
prepare the "copy," it being only two weeks. While
thus we feel that we have established a record as to
time, we have doubtless in our haste made our full

share of blunders, and so it is proposed to publish a supplement to this work which will be of much larger dimensions and contain the criticisms of those who haven't tried to issue an Annual.

Should your name be found among its leaves, think no more of it, and take the joke, if such is attached, in the spirit with which it is given.

To all those who have contributed in any way to the success of this volume we extend our hearty thanks. And now, Students, Faculty, Alumni, and Friends, we leave " The Grist " in your hands, hoping that it may meet with your favor and approval.

College Calendar for 1897-98.

1897.

Monday, April 5,	Spring Term begins at 1 P.M.
Friday, May 14,	Arbor Day.
Sunday, May 30, .	Memorial Day.
Monday, June 7,	Senior Examination begins.
Sunday, June 13. .	Baccalaureate Sermon.
Tuesday, June 15,	Commencement.
Saturday, June 19,	Entrance Examinations.
Wednesday, Sept. 1,	Entrance Examinations.
Monday, Sept. 20,	Entrance Examinations.
Tuesday, Sept. 21, .	Fall Term begins at 1 P.M.
	Thanksgiving Day.
Wednesday, Dec. 22,	Examinations begin.
Friday, Dec. 24, .	Term ends.

1898.

Monday, Jan. 3,	Winter Term begins at 1 P.M.
Wednesday, March 23,	Examinations begin.
Friday, March 25, .	Term ends.
Monday, April 4,	Spring Term begins at 1 P.M.
Sunday, June 12,	Baccalaureate Sermon.
Tuesday, June 14,	Term ends.

Board of Managers.

Corporation.

HON. MELVILLE BULL	. Newport County.
HON. C. H. COGGESHALL	. Bristol County.
HON. CHARLES J. GREENE	Washington County.
HON. HENRY L. GREENE	Kent County.
HON. GARDINER C. SIMS .	Providence County.

Officers of the Corporation.

HON. C. H. COGGESHALL, *President,*	. P. O., Bristol, R. I.
HON. HENRY L. GREENE, *Vice-President,*	P. O., Riverpoint, R. I.
HON. CHARLES J. GREENE, *Clerk,*	P. O., Kenyon, R. I.
HON. MELVILLE BULL, *Treasurer.*	P. O., Newport, R. I.

Faculty.

JOHN HOSEA WASHBURN, Ph. D.,

PRESIDENT.

Professor of Agricultural Chemistry.

B. S., Massachusetts Agricultural College, 1878; Graduate student, Brown University, 1880; Graduate student, Massachusetts Agricultural College, 1881-1883; Professor of Chemistry, Storrs Agricultural School, 1883-1887; Student in Göttingen University, 1885 and 1887-1889; Ph D., Göttingen, 1889; Appointed President, 1890.

CHARLES OTIS FLAGG, B.S.,

Emeritus Professor of Agriculture.

B. S., Massachusetts Agricultural College, 1872; President of Board of Managers of R. I. College of Agriculture and Mechanic Arts, 1888-1891; Professor of Agriculture, 1890-1896; Director of R. I. Experiment Station since 1889.

HOMER JAY WHEELER, Ph. D.,

Professor of Geology.

B. S., Massachusetts Agricultural College, 1883; Assistant Chemist, Massachusetts State Experiment Station, 1883-1887; Graduate student, University of Göttingen, 1887-1889; Ph. D., Göttingen, 1889 Appointed Chemist of R. I. Agricultural Experiment Station and Professor of Geology, 1890.

ANNE LUCY BOSWORTH, B.S.,

Professor of Mathematics.

B. S., Wellesley College, 1890; First Assistant, Amesbury (Mass.) High School, 1890-1892; Appointed Professor of Mathematics, April, 1892 Graduate student at the University of Chicago, summer of 1894 and 1896.

E. JOSEPHINE WATSON, A. M.,

Professor of Languages.

A. B., Smith College, 1881; A. M., The Cornell University, 1883; Assistant in English, Smith College, 1883-1887; Student of North European Languages in Göttingen, 1887-1889; Appointed Professor of Languages, September, 1891; Student of French in Tours, summer of 1895.

WILLIAM ELISHA DRAKE, B. S.,

Professor of Mechanical Engineering.

B. S., Polytechnic Institute, Worcester, 1886; Instructor in Physics and Electricity, Worcester Polytechnic Institute, 1887; Instructor in Woodworking at Pratt Institute, Brooklyn, 1887-1893; Appointed Professor of Mechanical Engineering, 1893.

OLIVER CHASE WIGGIN, M. D.,

Professor of Comparative Anatomy and Physiology.

M. D., Harvard University, 1866; Practicing physician in Providence, 1866-1886; Visiting physician to R. I. Hospital, 1872-1881; Consulting physician to Dexter Asylum, 1875-1885; President Providence Medical Association, 1880-1882; President Rhode Island Medical Society, 1884-1886; Founder of Providence Lying-in Hospital, and President, 1881-1891; Appointed Professor of Comparative Anatomy and Physiology, 1893.

WILLIAM WALLACE WOTHERSPOON,

Captain, 12th Infantry, U. S. A.,

Professor of Military Science and Tactics.

Appointed 2d Lieutenant, 12th Infantry, October 1, 1873; Promoted 1st Lieutenant, March 20, 1879; Promoted Captain 12th Infantry, April 28, 1891; Appointed Professor of Military Science and Tactics, November, 1894.

HARRIET LATHROP MERROW, A.M.,

Professor of Botany.

B. S., Wellesley College, 1886; Teacher of Science, Plymouth (Mass.) High School, 1887-1888; Teacher of Science, Harcourt Place, Gambier, O., 1888-1891; Graduate student, University of Michigan, 1891-1892; A. M., Wellesley College, 1893; Graduate assistant, Botanical Laboratory, University of Michigan, 1893-1894; Appointed Professor of Botany, January, 1895.

ARTHUR AMBER BRIGHAM, Ph. D.,

Professor of Agriculture.

B. S., Massachusetts Agricultural College, 1878; Engaged in practical farming, 1878-1888; Professor of Agriculture in the Imperial Agricultural College at Sapporo, Japan, 1888-1893; Graduate student at Göttingen University, 1893-1896; Ph. D., Göttingen, 1896; Appointed Professor of Agriculture, 1896.

GEORGE WILTON FIELD, Ph.D.,

Professor of Zoölogy.

A. B., Brown University, 1887, and A. M. 1890; Ph. D., Johns Hopkins University, 1892; Assistant in Biology, Johns Hopkins University, 1891-1892; Occupant of Smithsonian Table at Naples Zoölogical Station, 1892-1893; Student at University of Munich, 1893; Associate Professor of Cellular Biology, Brown University, 1893-1896; Appointed Professor of Zoölogy, 1896.

JAMES DE LOSS TOWAR, B. S.,

Assistant Professor of Agriculture and in Charge of Civil Engineering.

B. S., Michigan Agricultural College, 1885; Graduate Student at Michigan Agricultural College, 1890-1891; Assistant Agriculturist, R. I. Experiment Station, 1891-1894; Appointed Assistant Professor of Agriculture, R. I. College of Agriculture and Mechanic Arts, 1893; Appointed in Charge of Civil Engineering, 1895.

THOMAS CARROLL RODMAN,

Instructor in Woodwork.

Appointed, 1890.

MARY POWELL HELME,

Instructor in Drawing.

Student at Friends' School, Providence, R. I., 1879-1882; Associate Instructor in Drawing and Painting, Friends' School, 1883-1891; Appointed Instructor in Drawing, 1892; Pupil of Mrs. Rhoda Holmes Nichols, Augustus St. Gaudens, and William M. Chase.

ANNA BROWN PECKHAM, A. B.,

Instructor in Language and History.

A. B., Wellesley College, 1893; Instructor in Public School, Kingston, R. I., 1893-1894; Appointed Instructor in Languages and History, 1894.

ARTHUR CURTIS SCOTT, B. S.,

Instructor in Physics.

B. S., R. I. College of Agriculture and Mechanic Arts, 1895; Student at Harvard University, summer course in Physics, 1895; Appointed Instructor in Physics, 1895; Student at The Cornell University, summer course in Physics, 1896.

GEORGE BURLEIGH KNIGHT,

Instructor in Iron Work.

Appointed, 1896.

CHARLES SHERMAN CLARKE, B. S.,

Assistant in Mechanics,

B. S., R. I. College of Agriculture and Mechanic Arts, 1895; Appointed Assistant in Mechanics, 189

JOHN FRANKLIN KNOWLES, B. S.,

Instructor in Woodwork.

B. S., R. I. College of Agriculture and Mechanic Arts, 1894; Appointed Assistant in Mechanic 1894 ; Appointed Instructor in Woodwork, 1896.

LUCY HARRIET PUTNAM,

Instructor in Expression.

Graduate of School of Expression, Boston, Mass., 1896; Instructor at summer session of School Expression, Plymouth, Mass., 1896; Appointed Instructor in Expression, 1896.

CHARLES HENRY HOWARD STONE, B. S.,

Instructor in Chemisty.

B. S., Massachusetts Institute of Technology, 1896; Appointed Instructor in Chemistry, 189

HOWLAND BURDICK, B. S.,

Assistant in Agriculture.

B. S., R. I. College of Agriculture and Mechanic Arts, 1895; Appointed Assistant in Agriculture, 189

JOHN EDWARD HAMMOND, B. S.,

Assistant in Agriculture.

B. S., R. I. College of Agriculture and Mechanic Arts, 1895; Appointed Assistant in Agriculture, 189

CHARLES FRANKLIN KENYON,

Assistant in Chemistry.

NATHANIEL HELME,

Meteorologist.

The Ducking of Sergt. Williams.

JANUARY 12, 1896.

Mr. Williams, the largest man
  That ever walked the floor,
Was startled, Sunday evening,
  By a rap upon his door.

It sounded quite suspicious,
  So he stirred not from his chair;
But the club kept up its thumping
  Till he felt like pulling hair.

Then Sergt. Williams started
  On a trip among the boys
For the purpose to discover
  Who was making all the noise.

Now Sergt. Williams' passions
  To a shaky height arose ;
So he pulled off both his slippers
  And walked upon his toes.

He'd mounted to the second floor,
  Red-hot without and in,
And, had he been short-legged,
  He might have had to swim.

He collared Mr. Brightman,
  And said, "You go to-morrow";
Then down there came an ocean—
  Changing triumph into sorrow.

He jumped up to the third floor,
  All soaked from feet to head;
And, seizing Brother Palmer,
  He pulled him out of bed.

From here he went to Scott's room
  To tell of the affair—
To dry his regimentals
  And smooth his golden hair.

Now, we can't exactly calculate
  Just what the end will be;
But we think that Sergt. Williams
  Will fire two or three.

History.

IN 1863 the State of Rhode Island accepted from the United States Government the land grant scrip, which gave to each State thirty thousand acres of the public lands for each Senator and Representative in Congress. The land was to be sold by the States, the proceeds of the sale invested, and the income appropriated for the maintenance of at least one college where the leading object should be to teach such branches of learning as are related to Agriculture and Mechanic Arts.

By the Hatch Act of March 2, 1887, an annual appropriation of $15,000 was granted each State for the purpose of establishing an Agricultural Experiment Station in connection with an Agricultural College or School.

It was not until the summer of 1888, however, that the Rhode Island State Agricultural School was established, and in the meantime the funds for agricultural instruction had been appropriated by Brown University.

Further funds were granted the Agricultural Colleges by the new Morrill bill of August 30, 1890. That these might be used in Rhode Island the Agricultural School was incorporated as a college, and has been conducted on such a basis since September, 1892.

On April 19, 1894, the Legislature passed an act authorizing the State Treasurer to pay Brown University the sum of $40,000, in consideration of which the University was to turn over to the State the proceeds of the original Land Grant of 1862, and to withdraw from the United States Supreme Court its suit for the Morrill Fund.

The fire of January 27, 1895, destroyed the Dormitory, which was rebuilt, however, and ready for occupancy by the first of the following October.

During the past winter the Legislature appropriated $45,000 for a Drill and Recitation Hall. This building faces the centre of the prospective campus, and is already progressing well towards completion.

Such is a brief history of the College from a statistical standpoint. Its history from a student point of view is quite different. When the farm was purchased no substantial stone buildings ornamented it, though the ground was well sprinkled with rocks left by the glaciers of long ago. A multitude of little shanties surrounded the farm-house, which was gotten at only by means of a wretched road ; and it seemed as if a difficult job was in store for the officials of the new institution. But what a difference a few years made ! The roads were widened and improved, the shanties destroyed, the farm enlarged, and the farm-house painted. All these changes were made upon what had been. From granite quarried upon the place the Laboratory and College Hall were built, while the Boarding Hall and Mechanical Building were constructed of wood. Lawns were laid out and trees and shrubs planted.

The first class entered in September, 1890, before College Hall was fully completed. At that time the institution was a school with a three years' course, and so it continued to be until 1892.

In one tower of the first College Hall hung a bell, whose sweet tones called the students to meals, to chapel, and to class. The college history in the student's mind contains many pranks played with that same bell, whose last musical notes rang its own death-knell.

Another cherished memory of the earlier graduates is connected with the time when we became a college, and that inanimate thing, " Ben Butler," was so filled with joy that it burst.

One great trial to the students was the muddy, narrow path to the Hill, but this was banished several years ago in favor of a road, and a side-walk, which was the successful result of two " Bees."

The students have always been interested in Athletics, and will no doubt show greater interest when there are some facilities for gymnasium training.

The cadets, who had their first drill in 1894, are now organized into two companies, with efficient officers.

Thus far, the Commencement exercises have been held in a marquee on one of the lawns, but the building now under construction will contain a hall for such uses.

Although as a college we have encountered many trials, the future looks bright, and we feel confident of constantly increasing success. Our departments of study are already excellent, and with the steady advancement in standard and courses we expect to make our college one of the highest grade.

Questions.

Owing to lack of space the following questions can not bo answered until " our next."

Why are there not some new "cuts" in the catalogue?

Who built the bonfire that was charged to the Junior Class?

Who has got the "sporting blood"?

Why does it take some of the young men ten minutes to walk up to church and three-quarters of an hour to walk back again?

When will the girls get a new dormitory?

Who squeezed C——n's hand in the passageway?

Where is Huckamuck, and how large is it?

Who uses the hair-dye?

When are the Juniors going to get the ice-cream Doctor promised them?

What would happen if "Pat" fell upon "Levi"?

Mr. D——y, what is your name?

What becomes of the books, sweaters, and small change left in your room?

Why was the Chemical Laboratory so attractive to the Juniors last term?

"How many *ohms* are flowing through this wire?"

WOMEN'S DORMITORY.

The Classes.

" 1900."

CLASS COLOR : White.   CLASS FLOWER : White Rose.

CLASS YELL : Whoop-la-ra ! Whoop-la-re !
Walk up ! Chalk up ! Upside !
1900 ! Yes—sir-ee !

WE are only a class of Freshmen (but then all must have their turn at being Freshmen, and our boasting superiors have had theirs, but maybe they have forgotten it) and so our experience has been rather short and easily told.

To begin with,—it was the 16th day of September, 1896, that we began our career as collegians. How well I remember those first few days! Coming here among strangers it seemed as if there were three times as many students as there were; and every time I met one it seemed as if he must be a Senior, or at least a Junior. But that feeling soon disappeared. The grinding influence of Algebra wore off the corners, and the smoothing (?) influence of football polished things up so that all went as quietly as if oiled. (We did get watered sometimes). We heard various allusions to the "goose-eggs," "double oits," etc.; but when we came to chase the goose-egg with the Sophs, and South Kingstown High School,— well, never mind, we know all about it! We also know what the professors have said about our marks, as compared with those of the last year's Freshmen.

This is a very enterprising class, for before the second term had gone by it brought some very popular things into the College. As one after another was missed from his accustomed place it was whispered, "He's got 'em." A discussion arose in an English recitation as to whether it was not more correct to say, "He's got *it*." Those who had "*'em*," however, were not much in doubt. Because of these mysterious things, great interest was taken in examinations. "Have you passed in your Book-keeping?" "Did you pass the Algebra exam. ?"—were questions heard on every side.

As I said before, we are only a class of Freshmen, but we propose to keep climbing, and, as the renowned somebody-or-other from somewhere once said, "We'll see you later."   J. R. E.

Freshman Class.

Officers.

A. PEARSON, President.
    Miss S. L. JAMES, Vice-President.
        Miss B. D. TUCKER, Secretary.
            A. E. MUNRO, Treasurer.

Honorary Member.

Miss Lucy H. Putnam,   Newton, Mass.

Members.

Latham Clarke,	West Kingston.
Morton Robinson Cross,	Wakefield.
John Raleigh Eldred,	Kingston.
John James Fry,	East Greenwich.
Prescott Morrill Greene,	Peace Dale.
Ruth Hortense James,	Kenyon.
Sara Lila James,	Kenyon.
Charles Andrew Jollie,	Providence.
Amos Langworthy Kenyon,	Wood River Junction.
Alston Windfield Knowles,	Point Judith.
Leroy Weston Knowles,	Point Judith.
Elisha Frederic Lanphear,	Peace Dale.
Arthur Earle Munro,	Quonochontaug.
Abbie Fidelia Northup,	Wickford.
Elizabeth May Parkhurst,	Wickford.
Alfred Pearson,	Newburyport, Mass.
Oscar Dean Sherman,	Wickford.
Robert Joseph Sherman,	Usquepaug.
Borden Lawton Sisson,	South Portsmouth.
Marion Sumner Sisson,	South Portsmouth.
George Canning Soule,	Wickford.
Ralph Nelson Soule,	Wickford.
Anthony Enoch Steere,	Chepachet.
Lenora Estelle Stillman,	Kenyon.
Bertha Douglass Tucker,	Swansea Centre, Mass.
Herbert Comstock Wells,	Kingston.
Chester Wilson Whitman,	Arctic.
Levi Eugene Wightman,	South Scituate.
Joseph Robert Wilson,	Allenton.

'99.

CLASS COLORS : Blue and Salmon-Pink.

CLASS YELL : R. I. C. We are thine !
The noble class of '99. Rah !

CLASS MOTTO : Originality and Integrity.

We have crossed the awful chasm,
And are on the other shore.
Freshman, don't you look so gloomy –
Some day you'll be a Sophomore.

A S I start to write this brief sketch, a momentary comparison of the classes of '99 and 1900 passes before me, and I can truthfully and thankfully say that, whatever appearances may have been, we can never be accused of being quite so verdant as the nineteen-hundredites.

We do not wish to give anyone the impression that we are at all vain ; but, having been so successful in all class games, the enumeration of which I shall forbear, as the shame and mortification of our elders would be too great, we feel, at least, as though we had nothing in this line of which to be ashamed. We regret that the Freshmen have been too timid to venture forth with canes. We feel confident as to the result.

Always striving for originality, this Spring we elected one of our lady members manager of the ball team, and we are glad to say that the experiment has proved very satisfactory.

With one or two exceptions our first year of college life was the same as that of any class. These exceptions are well worthy of mention. After the fire a new drill shed was required. Always ready to respond in a time of need, we built the present drill shed, and we beg to state that this feat has never been equalled before nor since.

Time passed, and we were happy, for we thought of the days when we should be Sophomores, and we made up our minds to treat the Freshmen as the Sophomores had treated us. Did we do it? Ask the Freshmen!

The Fall term came, and, drawn closer together by the withdrawal of some of our members, we determined "to do or die." With almost perfect success we passed through the mysteries of Trig., and bid fair to conquer the dreaded foe, Chemistry.

As a whole, our Sophomore year has been a pleasant one—brightened by our many happy class meetings and social gatherings.

Our honorary member, Miss A. B. Peckham, has always been a help and pleasure to the class, and has done much to bring us into closer fellowship with one another.

> And now, kind friends, we'll say adieu,
> With hopes next year of greeting you—
> Our history, then, will all be new,
> From the historian of the Sophomores true.

H. F. W. A.

Sophomore Class.

Officers.

H. F. W. ARNOLD, PRESIDENT.

MISS PIERCE, VICE-PRESIDENT.

MISS HARVEY, SECRETARY.

H. M. BRIGHTMAN, TREASURER.

Honorary Member.

MISS ANNA B. PECKHAM, .   *Kingston.*

Members.

NATHANIEL BERTRAM ALLEN,	. . . *Pawtuxet.*
EVERETT MULLEN ARNOLD, . .	*Wood River Junction.*
HENRY FRANCIS WALLING ARNOLD, .	*Woonsocket.*
WILLIAM STANHOPE BACHELLER,	*Newport.*
HENRY MAXON BRIGHTMAN,	*White Rock.*
JAMES EDWARD CARGILL, .	. *Abbott Run.*
JOHN STUART CUMMING, .	. *Pawtucket.*
ROBERT STANLEY DOUGHTY,	*Providence.*
MILDRED WAYNE HARVEY, .	. . . *Allenton.*
BLYDON ELLERY KENYON,	*Wood River Junction.*
CARROLL KNOWLES,	. *Kingston.*
HARRY KNOWLES, . .	. . . *Point Judith.*
MERRILL AUGUSTUS LADD, .	. *Bay Shore, Long Island.*
WILLIAM FRAZIER OWENS,	*Cannonsville, N. Y.*
EBENEZER PAYNE, .	. *Lyons Farms, N. J.*
WALTER CLARK PHILLIPS,	. *Lafayette.*
NELLIE HOLLIS PIERCE,	*Malden, Mass.*
ROBERT SPINK REYNOLDS,	*Wickford.*
MINNIE ELIZABETH RICE,	. . *Wickford.*
GEORGE ALBERT SHERMAN,	*West Kingston.*
SALLY RODMAN THOMPSON, .	. *Wakefield.*

JUNIOR CLASS.

'98.

ON the eighteenth of September, 1894, we, as nearly thirty timid Freshmen, attended chapel at Kingston for the first time. We entered as the largest class Kingston had ever known and were destined to become one of the most enterprising. Within ten days our first class-meeting was held, and in a few weeks our pins arrived.

Military drill was introduced in November, though the uniforms did not appear until almost January. Those of us who were then awkward privates have risen in the ranks, until now our class can boast of its two lieutenants, its first sergeant, and many other officers of lesser rank.

We were progressing gaily through the dewy period when came the fire of January twenty-seventh, which deprived us of our much cherished college home, and forced us to resort to Barracks and long-distance walking for nearly two terms. Despite the gloom and anxiety which this fire caused, we paused to smile over the funny incidents connected with it. One man—no longer with us— confused, paused before his mirror at the last moment to comb his hair. Another, anxious to save what he could, leaned from his window to toss his mirror down to the grass. Needless to say, there was not enough left for souvenirs even. We remember also that one Freshman gave the alarm of fire on the Hill that day, and another distinguished himself upon the roof of the Boarding Hall at a time when that building was in imminent danger.

June came, and we rejoiced to be Sophomores. Shortly after the Fall term opened, class canes were secured, which added much to our feeling of independence. During this year the class was divided in most studies, as we were too many for a teacher to instruct all at once.

On Arbor Day—May first—our class tree, a rock maple, was

planted. True to the character of our class, the exercises at that time were most original—a great addition being found in the assistance of Miss Bosworth, who, a few days later, honored us in becoming a member of our class. We wished her to wear our pin, so surprised her on a night in June and presented her with one.

June thirteenth saw the gayest time that ever came to '98. A long day spent on the sands at Wesquage Beach was exceedingly pleasant, although all suffered from the sun's hot rays. The strolls across the rocks, the washing of ice-cream dishes, the games upon the sand, all offered amusement suited to the various tastes of the crowd.

In a few days came the rush of Commencement, and soon the last deeds were done and we were Juniors, with memories of salutes and bonfires in the far-away Sophomore days.

We began our activity as the Junior class with our reception to the new students, which was a great success.

During the Fall and Winter, Chemistry was our great bug-bear. We had many teachers, and our pathway was rocky indeed. We were sufficiently alive, however, to bid Qualitative a joyful farewell at the end of the term.

Later came the Grist, and reception to the Seniors, which closed the year fittingly.

All through our college course we have manifested a strong class spirit which, added to our numbers, has helped us to accomplish great things.

The class has shown a deep interest in athletics, many of our members having taken prominent places on the base-ball and foot-ball teams; while in all entertainments given by the Association the young ladies of the class have rendered generous help.

The traditional characteristics of the Junior have not been lacking among us. At times a gloomy face or anxious brow has indicated some fleeting disappointment, but we hope to pass on into Senior year with our number no further depleted.

This brief sketch hints at what '98 has done ; what it will do is veiled in dim future ; but all its deeds, if like the past, will be noteworthy.

We submit this history to you, our friends, and beg you will be gentle critics—for you, too, may sometime fall into the joys and temptations of a Junior's life.   M. R. F.

Junior Class.

Officers.

W. C. CLARKE, President.

A. A. TUCKER, Vice-President.

Miss WELLS, Secretary.

A. A. TUCKER, Treasurer.

Honorary Member.

Miss Anne L. Bosworth,   *Kingston.*

Members.

Sarah Estelle Arnold,	*Wakefield.*
George Washington Barber,	*Shannock.*
Edna Maria Cargill,	*Abbott Run.*
John P. Case,	*Gould.*
William Case Clarke,	*Wakefield.*
William Lamont Wheeler Clarke,	*Jamestown.*
Henry Augustus Congdon,	*Kingston.*
Martha Rebecca Flagg,	*Kingston.*
William Ferguson Harley,	*Pawtucket.*
Henry Francis O'Neil,	*Providence.*
George Tucker Rose,	*Kingston.*
Abbie Gertrude Sherman,	*Kingston.*
Robert Bruce Strout,	*Wakefield.*
William James Taylor,	*Mendon, Mass.*
Attmore Arnold Tucker,	*Wakefield.*
Harriette Florence Turner,	*Ontario Centre, N. Y.*
Grace Perry Wells,	*Kingston.*
Grace Ellen Wilson,	*Allenton.*
Silas Wilber Wright,	*Wakefield.*

'97.

" When we first came on this campus,
Freshmen were we—green as grass :
Now, as grave and reverend Seniors,
Smile we o'er our verdant past."

MANY times in former years we have been in chapel and heard Prexy say, " The Seniors will please remain, the others are excused." That was when we were under-classmen, and we knew that the unfortunate Seniors were having a small curtain lecture on " Dignity as Reflected by Our Senior Class." We are happy, and also extremely fortunate, to be able to say that we have never had to be addressed on that subject. In the opinion of one Freshman, " The Seniors are sadly lacking in dignity." Others have not, as a rule, ventured to express their views on the matter.

We were delightfully surprised at the beginning of the year to find that our numbers had been increased. Two young ladies who had entered on short courses had their work in such shape as to be able to graduate in June with us. We are a very different class than we were in the Fall of '93, when we first came to Kingston. Only four of the original class are left. The others have departed for parts unknown, and we very seldom see them. But " there is no great loss without some small gain," and our new members have more than made up for those we have lost.

Ninety-seven is remarkably proficient in two things : the first is cutting chapel ; the second, getting those cuts excused in order to cut again. Beside this remarkable accomplishment, we have one other redeeming feature. The progress we make in Mechanics is simply astonishing, especially on those days when " Prof. Willie " is detained from class.

Of course we have our " curios," as has every other class. There is the absent-minded young man who forgets to take off his skates when he leaves the pond with a young lady, but we think he will ougrow this. Then there is another young man who has defied the Doctors, Death, and most of the rest of us, by taking a six-hour course in " dying." What is most remarkable is, he seems to suffer no evil effects from it. Then we have one of our number on the Faculty! Assistant in Chemistry, just think of that! We did not know this until the 1897 Catalogue came out, and the dignity and honor of the class have been raised about two hundred and ninety-seven per cent. by the announcement. There was once a young lady in our class whose remarkable feature was an extreme fond-ness for sitting in a hammock with a young man; but, alas, she has left us. As a masher, one of the fellows thinks he is " in it," as he " cuts ice " in various quarters. But—" Let him that think-eth he standeth take heed lest he fall."

Some of the class elect Astronomy and like to study the stars, but the Faculty have made a rule that if the class wish to study the stars they must go in groups larger than two, and—star-gazing has lost its attractions.

Ninety-seven has never been prominent in athletics. The centre-rush of our last foot-ball team was a ninety-seven man, and after the season's defeats were over he remarked cheerfully, " I must have been a Jonah to the rest of the team."

And now, as our course is nearly ended, we look back at the years we have passed here and think how pleasant they have been. It will be with great regret that we turn our backs on our friends in Kingston and in the Rhode Island College, while for those " down below "—the less said the better. " Alas, the best of friends must part." A. F. G.

Senior Class.

Officers.

I. THOMAS, PRESIDENT.

A. P. KENYON, VICE-PRESIDENT.

H. E. B. CASE, SECRETARY.

MISS HANSON, TREASURER.

A. F. GRINNELL, HISTORIAN.

Executive Committee.

W. S. CARMICHAEL,   MISS TEFFT,   C. F. KENYON.

Members.

WELCOME SANDS CARMICHAEL,	*Shannock.*
HERBERT EDWARDS BROWN CASE,	*Pawtucket.*
ARCHIE FRANKLIN GRINNELL.	*Middletown.*
GERTRUDE MAIE HANSON, .	*. Peace Dale.*
BESSIE BAILEY HOXSIE, .	*Quonochontaug.*
JESSIE LOUISE LARKIN,	*Westerly.*
CHARLES FRANKLIN KENYON, .	*Shannock.*
ALBERT PRENTICE KENYON,	*. Ashaway.*
LOUIS HERBERT MARSLAND,	*Franklin, N. Y.*
ELIZA ALICE TEFFT, .	*Allenton.*
IRVING THOMAS, .	*Lafayette.*

Specials.

MARGARET BALDWIN,	*Aspen Wall, Va.*
ALFRED WILSON BOSWORTH,	*Boston, Mass.*
BENJAMIN CARPENTER, .	*. Perryville.*
HAROLD WARREN CASE,	*Pawtucket.*
EDMUND DANIEL CULLEN,	*. Wickford.*
FRANK ROFFEE EDDY,	*Providence.*
JAMES R. EMMETT, .	*Peace Dale.*
GERTRUDE SARAH FISON, .	*. Peace Dale.*
WILLIAM CHAUNCEY PALMER MERRILL,	*Central Falls.*
CLIFFORD BREWSTER MORRISON,	*Pawtucket.*
CLARENCE EARL NASH, .	*Watch Hill.*
ROENA HOXSIE STEERE,	*Wood River Junction.*
HARRY PAGE WILSON,	*. Allenton.*

Our Class Tree.

PLANTED ARBOR DAY, MAY 1, 1896.

———

Here our class tree we will plant,
  And if Nature's hand does treat it well,
It will stand to show the ignorant,
  That in knowledge we excel.

This maple was the tree we chose,
  A tree of beauty not surpassed.
When our tree takes root and grows,
  A pleasant shade its boughs will cast.

It is an honor to our class;
  A memory that will stand to show,
When we from college life have passed,
  That here in knowledge we did grow.

When other classes follow us,
  On the road to knowledge,
Our tree will then be vigorous
  And a pride to Kingston College.

Beneath its boughs the student
  In pleasant days of June,
If he is not imprudent,
  Will keep his mind in tune.

Many a feathery guest will come
   And make this tree his home,
The studious girl and her college chum
   To its pleasant shade will roam.

As time rolls on at Kingston,
   Other trees here will grow;
But this one, its life well begun,
   The broadest shade will throw.

Who can say but some fine day,
   Beneath this tree we'll meet
And hold a class reunion gay,
   And all our old friends greet.

Long live this tree of ninety-eight's,
   May it receive praises loud,
That we whom it commemorates,
   May of our tree be proud.

Classified Facts.

Name.	Characteristics.	Favorite Occupation.	Highest Ambition.	Matrimonial Prospects.
THOMAS, I.	A man of muscle	Smoking.	To dye	Bright.
CASE, H. E. D.	Standing like a soldier.	Studying.	To grow tall	Uncertain.
MARSLAND, L. H.	He has hair	Entertaining	To be a Major-General	Fair.
KENYON, C. F.	Precipitated in fifth group.	Cleaning the acid from his coat	To be a Remsen.	Unknown substance.
GRINNELL, A. F.	A Green-man.	Curling his hair.	To play a bugle	On good foundation.
CUMMING, J. S.	Johnny loves to drill.	Caring for his uniform.	To jump	Black.
SHERMAN, Miss A.	A Ben-jay-man's-friend.	Analysis of H_2O	To marry	Too young.
BALDWIN, Miss M.	Her love for apples	Dancing a jig.	To become an R.I. greening	Stunning.
TURNER, Miss H. F.	Frivolous	Winking at the boys in chapel.	To sell white gloves.	Turning.
STILLMAN, Miss L. E.	Trivial	Flirting on the train.	To become speedy	Uncounted
CLARKE, W. L. W.	A lad of gumption.	Experimenting with X rays	To get a shock	Unbiased
DOUGHTY, R. S.	Naughty.	Sleeping until seven-thirty	To be a minister.	Way up.
O'NEIL, H. F.	A deep thinker	Studying the origin of man.	To find the missing link	Minus.
SHERMAN, R. J.	He is a romancer	Telling bear stories	To extinguish animal life.	On the wing.
CULLEN, E. D.	Not to be published	Umpiring the game	To take life easy.	Sehr gut.

Our Alma Mater.

———

IF, in the few words written of the Rhode Island College of Agriculture and Mechanic Arts, I may express in a measure the large debt of gratitude I owe this institution, or influence some reader to take advantage of the opportunities it offers, I shall be grateful for the privilege.

One regrets that the world holds a college training as useless that does not make a professor of every student. In truth, mankind is prone to criticise the graduate as though he were a " finished product," without reference to the " raw material " he presented when he entered.

It is evident that there is a great difference in the personal equations of the students who enter any of the colleges, but especially is it true of those admitted to the Agricultural and Mechanical Colleges.

The only fair estimate of the advantages of a college training, is the one that takes account of the improvement made in the mind and body of the student during the four or more years he is under the college discipline.

According to this estimate I believe that the Rhode Island College of Agriculture and Mechanic Arts stands on a par with any similar institution and many classical colleges in this country. True it does not make the specialist, but it does more,—it gives a general practical education ; a basis for any life in any place.

This college occupies a unique position among the educational institutions of this State; because it appeals to a growing generation of boys and girls who desire a higher education and who cannot afford to attend the classical colleges.

That a college education has its disadvantages is a prevalent impression that has recently found expression in an article entitled, "Drawbacks of a College Education," in the *Forum* of December, 1896.

The four principal drawbacks considered were:

1st. "The tendency of a college education to promote a love for the agreeable. The college may minister to an indolence manifesting itself in methods at once gentle and inane, of excellent form, but worthless content."

2d. "Training the judgment of a student at the expense of his energy."

3d. "The time spent in getting a college education removes the man destined for a commercial life from the most favorable opportunities for learning business."

4th. "That the college fills the mind with useless knowledge and trains it in antiquated methods of thought and action."

The happy combination of the practical and theoretical in the curriculum of the Rhode Island College of Agriculture and Mechanic Arts makes it peculiarly free from these somewhat generally recognized drawbacks. The number of hours of recitation a day required of the regular student, and the practical application of the principle taught, preclude any probability of fostering an excessive love of the agreeable.

The training of the judgment is not liable to be at the expense of the energy, where the physical well-being of a student receives proper attention. In regard to the loss of time in attending college, preventing a student from getting an early start in business, I firmly believe that the increased knowledge of the laws which govern material, and especially the improvement in the command of language, outweigh all the advantages accruing from an early footing in business.

The fourth drawback does not apply to the College of Agriculture and Mechanic Arts, as what is called " useless information " usually refers to the study of the dead languages, and "antiquated methods" to the study of ancient history and philosophy, which are either optional or absent in these courses.

I would speak more at length of the comparative positions of the graduates from Agricultural and Classical colleges, because so many people labor under the impression that the Agricultural student has acquired only a few theories which refer to the constituents of fertilizers, principles of stock-breeding, and manipulation of the plow, and express no little surprise at finding him conversant with French and German.

Now it is evident that what might be called the accomplishments are just as useful, or decorative, to the graduate of an Agricultural as a Classical college, and as the opportunities are equal, there is no reason why they should not be equally proficient.

The Rhode Island College of Agriculture and Mechanic Arts affords a better course and better facilities for the study of chemistry, both organic and inorganic, than do the classical colleges ; and in botany in the Agricultural, and mathematics in the Mechanical course, the opportunities are equal or superior to the average college. After all, with all the advantages of an institution, it is still very dependent upon the interest of its students for its best success.

Missionaries from Alaska tell us that the young Alaskans promise if their kind visitors will teach them, they will work the rest of their lives for them. If only some of this thirst for knowledge could be infused into the boys and girls of Rhode Island, our State college would have more material of which to make good citizens.

The capacity for appreciating intellectual things is in direct proportion to the time invested in study, and for this reason it is of vital importance that the young men and women seize every opportunity of training their minds.

The acquisition of an intense desire for good literature is the priceless heritage of the graduate. He has the rest of his life in which to satiate this longing.

It does for him, what James Russell Lowell in one of his first essays entitled, "The Functions of a Poet," says that the poet does for us. "The poet is he who gives us those key words, the possession of which makes us masters of all the unsuspected treasure caverns of thought and feeling and beauty which open under the dusty paths of our daily life."

This increase in our ability to understand and enjoy the commonplace in life, this revealing all that is beautiful in nature, must be classed among the treasures that moth and rust do not corrupt, nor thieves break in and steal.

To-day a college training is indispensable for one who wishes to enter competition in business, or follow a profession.

I think it no depreciation of the advantages of the Rhode Island College to call it a preparatory school for life. It takes hold of the latent possibilities in a student, first makes him aware of them, then tells him how to use them; confers upon him the power of using material things, and develops his mental faculties, meanwhile constantly instilling into him honesty, integrity, manliness. Finally he is sent out. A finished product? Of necessity not, but with a generous improvement on the original. He goes with power which he can use for good or evil; but in his heart is this final unwritten injunction:

"Whatsoever things are true, whatsoever things are honest, whatsoever things are just, whatsoever things are pure, whatsoever things are lovely, whatsoever things are of good report; if there be any virtue, and if there be any praise, think on these things."

GENERAL VIEW BEFORE THE FIRE.

In Memoriam.

———

There was quiet at the College,
That clear January morn
As the sun rose o'er the hill-top,
Waking up the boys at dawn.
Gleaming in the eastern windows,
Filling every heart with cheer,
And perchance increasing interest
In our transient home so dear.

We on this as other Sundays,
Who were glad to lie till late,
Heeded not the first bell's clamor,
Waited till it tinkled eight.
But the tinkling had its meaning,
Even as in times before,
When it rung for us "a college,"
And more money at the door.

Soon we rose to heed its summons,
Stopping not for house-work then;
But repaired at once to breakfast,
Sure we'd have it done by ten.
Ten o'clock for such was church time,
For all those who liked to walk,
Or sought another service,
Than is found in Kingston talk.

But we boys the larger portion
Went to service on the Hill:
Seeking with the morning brightness,
All our straight backed pews to fill.
Welcoming back our pastor,
With his snowy locks once more,
As for two weeks he'd been absent
With grim illness at his door.

But he soon was anchored firmly,
And his text would fain expound,
When a herald rushed upon us,
Yet could hardly speak a sound.
Breathlessly in he rattled
While we looked around in ire,
Paling at his whispered message,
" The College is all afire."

Right quick the alarm was given.
And the people faced about,
Leaving the astonished parson.
To watch them going out.
But the preacher also followed
When the awful news he heard ;
While the boys rushed for the College
Never stopping for a word.

In the meantime those at College.
Who no church unto did go,
Had fought and fought the horrid flames
In the building high and low.
Some there were who got excited,
Rushing up the stairs and down ;
Shouting out, " Get pails!" " Get water!"
" Ring the bell and raise the town !"

But the flames were overpowering,
With no fire department nigh,
And as we rushed the hill adown,
We saw smoke rolling high.
And when at last no human power
The building then could save,
We rushed for valuables, and sought
The stifling smoke to brave.

The fire raged fiercely at the roof,
Burning thence its way below,
Thus allowing all the workers,
Time to gather ere it go.
Everything was hurled at random,
Through made openings to the ground,
While the Wakefield pickaninnies,
Picked things up when they came round.

"Hi, look out there! What ye doing?"
Shouts old Wilcox, turning red,
As a box flies out the window,
Smacks him crack upon the head.
"Catch this mirror," shouts another,
As he holds it on a string,
And the fellow far beneath it,
Steps aside and lets it ring.

Then from out a front wall window,
Comes a trunk and washbowl down ;
Filled alike with poultry relics
And mementoes of the town.
But the drop was too disastrous,
For crockery of this brand,
As the owner found it later,
With a pillow in his hand.

And out went the bureaus likewise,
With the mattresses on top,
While banjo heads and necks were broken
In obedience to the drop.
Till soon the lawn was covered ;
And 'twas good that such was so,
For in half an hour, the place inside
No mortal man could go.

The wind from the west was blowing,
And the fire raged fiercely on ;
With only an hour for our seeing
Our beautiful building gone.
But when alas, our hopes are bubbles,
Then can we know our friends ;
And great is the gratitude heartfelt,
Toward him who assistance lends.

Our friends were found in the village
Who housed us here and there ;
That we might continue at College,
And not give up in despair.
To them we owe all honor
For their kindness in our need ;
And may such wilful giving
Always surely gain its meed.

But chaos followed such disaster,
As our fire about had brought ;
Each one seeking out his trinkets,
Finding other than he sought.
The faculty well of course could manage
Even this calamity so vast,
And with rescued apparatus
Led us on again at last.

Books were piled in all directions,
We recited everywhere,
Yet with cheerful hearts we did it,
Glad that we were even there.
Glad we weren't awakened
In the middle of the night,
To escape the fiery fury,
All our senses dazed with fright.

As soon as order was restored
And all was started right,
The excavation work began
Among the ruined sight.
Various things were resurrected
By the boys for relics rare,
Such as kettles, thimbles, sewing tackle,
Andirons and an iron square.

But the thing most longed and sought for,
Was the dear old College bell,
That was to us so precious,
We wondered where it fell.
And longed to see it yet entire
But it too had gone, alas,
Like many other cherished things,
Through fire compelled to pass.

The old bell now is melted,
And hushed its iron tongue,
But we'll class it with " Ben Butler,"
In our memories ever young.
And as we greet the future, for nobler ends to try,
We'll ne'er forget our College, but keep its precepts nigh,
And lend to its good influence,
Which, please God may never die.

General Calendar.

1896.

Sept. 16. College opens.

18. Great excitement among the Freshmen during the evening.

21. "Gump" squares the circle by multiplying it by itself.

23. First lesson in Qualitative.

25. "Capt." Bates displays great bravery in putting out the fire at the Mechanical Building.

28. Soule gets the mumps.

Oct. 1. Physical examination by "Sergt." Brightman.

3. Leap-year straw-ride to Matunuck Beach.

6. Morrison receives a note from the girls.

7. Dr. W. has an heir.

20. Standard percentage raised.

24. The Juniors give a reception to the new students.

Nov. 3. Election Day. No exercises.

25. Strout determines the following law : "The molecular weight of the given substance, all-of-it, is to the molecular weight of the required substance, whole-of-it, as the actual weight of the given substance, some-of-it, to the actual weight of the required substance, none-of-it."

Dec. 3. Dr. doesn't appear in time for Chemistry.

8. Heavy showers in the dormitory.

11. Exeunt water-throwers.

22. Term closes.

GENERAL VIEW WITH COLLEGE HALL REBUILT.

1897.

Jan. 3. Winter term begins. O'Neil fails to appear.

8. Boston Tech. throws a Stone at the College.

12. Young ladies requested to remain after chapel exercises.

14. Miss Merrow gives the girls a lecture.

15. Measles appear at Watson House.

28. Day of Prayer for Colleges. Snow a foot deep.

31. No. 33 is quarantined.

Feb. 3. A measles card on the dormitory.

5. The General Assembly grant $45,000 for the building of a Drill Hall.

23. Darkness falls upon Kingston—no gas. Sleigh rides.

Mar 4. McKinley. Tucker becomes big enough to go to meeting barefooted.

23. Nine Juniors spend the evening on a Qual. exam.

26. Term ends. Qualitative is over.

Apr. 5. College re-opens. Carmichael begins **to be regular in** his attendance at chapel.

6. Work on new Drill Hall is begun.

15. Blondy's new wheel has arrived.

22. Invasion of Girls' Room by the Sophs.

May 3. Miss Bosworth receives her classmates in the evening.

4. First practice of the Watson House base-ball nine.

5. Meeting of the Chaucer Club announced in chapel.

11. Dr. umpires a ball game.

14. Seniors and Juniors play base-ball. Junior reception to the Seniors.

18. Cunning at drill in full uniform.

Arbor Day Song.

MAY 1, 1896.

O Nature's sweet day,
  O noontide of Spring,
With gladness we greet thee,
  Thy praises we sing.
For earth in its beauty,
  This fair month of May,
Grows brighter with gifts,
  Bestowed on this day.

We bring to thy bosom,
  O sweet Mother Earth,
Our tree, our remembrance
  Of Arbor Day's birth.
And here on the hillside,
  Rhode Island shall claim,
Our class tree, the maple,
  Of ancestral fame.

We'll watch it advance,
  And rise towards the sun,
As upward, still upward,
  Each new height is won.
Though hard be its pathway,
  'Twill toil day and night,
For Nature is Progress,
  And Progress is Might.

The future's before us,
  On, on we must go,
We'll meet many trials,
  We'll face many a foe.
Let us take for example,
  Our firm patient tree,
For Nature's its teacher,
  She's wiser than we,

♣

The Clubs.

♣

Zoölogical Club.

THE Zoölogical Club meets bi-weekly for the study of the local fauna, for the presentation of brief papers, and for the review of current journals. A special room is devoted to the collections and preparations made by the Club. The daily observations by the members upon the occurrence, habitat, structure, life history, and habits, of the animals, are on file for ready reference. Special excursions are made to favorable localities. Opportunities for field work in Zoölogy are remarkably fine.

Zoölogical Club.

Officers.

H. F. O'NEIL, President.

H. F. TURNER, Vice-President.

H. KNOWLES, Secretary.

E. PAYNE, Curator.

Members.

Miss Peckham,	Miss Putnam,
Miss McCrillis,	Miss Baldwin,
Dr. Field,	Dr. Wiggin,
C. P. Morrison,	J. J. Fry,
R. S. Reynolds,	N. B. Allen,
A. Pearson,	H. M. Brightman.

Chemical Club.

———

THE Chemical Club meets once in two weeks for the purpose of discussing the literature upon Chemical, Physical
and Agricultural subjects. The French, German, and
English journals are distributed among the members, and reports
are received from time to time on subject-matter from thirty-five
different journals.

Chemical Club.

Officers.

C. F. KENYON, President.

W. J. TAYLOR, Vice-President.

H. W. ARNOLD, Secretary.

Members.

Dr. Washburn,	Dr. Wheeler,
Dr. Field,	Prof. Scott,
Prof. Stone,	Prof. Towar,
B. L. Hartwell,	C. L. Sargent,
H. Knowles,	C. B. Morrison,
H. F. O'Neil,	Miss Baldwin.

Miss Bosworth.

Botanical Club.

———

In Charge of the Professor of Botany.

———

THOSE interested in botanical subjects meet occasionally to discuss botanical literature, especially the bulletins of the Experiment Stations and of the United States Government. Excursions are occasionally taken to favorable places.

The Associations.

Y. M. C. A.

———

THE Association at the College was founded May 29, 1894, to promote growth in grace and Christian fellowship among the students. The Association consists of students who are of good moral character. Weekly meetings are held at which different subjects of interest to the students are discussed. Our Association is a branch of the Intercollegiate movement and we are represented by one or more delegates every year at the Student's Conference at Northfield. It is the purpose of the Association to seek out all new students and bring them into Christian fellowship with its members.

Y. M. C. A.

Officers.

M. A. LADD, President.

W. F. HARLEY, Vice-President.

W. E. DRAKE, Cor. Secretary.

W. P. ALEXANDER, Rec. Secretary.

E. A. BATES, Treasurer.

Athletic Association.

THE Athletic Association was formed in 1892 for the promotion of Athletics at the College. Recently the Association has been reorganized, a constitution adopted, and the whole established on a firmer footing. There being no field athletics as yet, the Association has charge of base ball and foot ball, both of which it has promoted.

Athletics have never in the past been any too well supported by the students or faculty, and perhaps our teams have met with more than their share of defeats. The causes of this are not hard to find. The lack of a gymnasium has been a prime factor, which, however, is soon to be remedied ; and in the building now in course of construction, we shall have a gymnasium of which we may well be proud. Another very evident reason is the short time devoted to practice by the players, especially if the preceding game has been won. A third cause, which will be still more apparent with our new gymnasium, is the lack of a physical instructor ; one not only capable of teaching the proper use of the apparatus, but competent to coach the base ball and foot ball teams as well.

The want of interest manifested in the past by many of the undergraduates is deplorable ; but what incentive is there for a man to try for any team when he knows that his opponents will have been far better trained and grounded in the game than himself?

The recent revival of interest in sports by the Faculty is gratifying and cannot fail to stimulate the lagging efforts of some of the students. Already our fields no longer present the almost deserted appearance they once did at the hour of practice, and if we only persist, our teams may have better success, and the " R. I. C." be made to mean more than ever before in Athletics.

Athletic Association.

Officers.

W. J. TAYLOR, President.

W. C. CLARKE, Vice-President.

H. E. B. CASE, Secretary.

W. F. OWENS, Treasurer.

W. F. OWENS, Manager.

Foot Ball Team.

W. C. CLARKE,   CAPTAIN.

E. D. CULLEN, .	. . Full Back.
W. C. P. MERRILL,	Half Back.
R. S. DOUGHTY,	. Half Back.
W. C. CLARKE,	. Quarter Back.
I. THOMAS,	. Centre.
W. F. HARLEY,	. Right Guard.
J. R. EMMET, .	. Left Guard.
W. S. CARMICHAEL,	Right Tackle.
H. P. WILSON,	. Left Tackle.
B. CARPENTER,	Right End.
H. W. CASE,	Left End.

Substitutes :

A. PEARSON, JR.,   C. E. NASH.

FOOTBALL TEAM.

Polo Team.

W. C. P. MERRILL,   CAPTAIN.

R. S. DOUGHTY,   Goal.
W. C. P. MERRILL,   Rusher.
H. P. WILSON,   . Rusher.
E. D. CULLEN,   Half Back.
R. S. REYNOLDS,   . Centre.

Substitutes:

C. A. JOLLIE,   J. R. WILSON.

Base Ball Team.

H. P. WILSON,   CAPTAIN.

COLLEGE NINE.

Battery:

W. C. P. MERRILL,   , Pitcher.
W. F. OWENS,   Catcher.

In-Field:

H. P. WILSON,   First Base.
A. A. TUCKER,   Second Base.
C. S. JOLLIE, .   Third Base.
R. S. REYNOLDS,   Short Stop.

Out-Field:

W. C. CLARKE,   . Right Field.
J. J. FRY,   Centre Field.
M. R. CROSS, .   Left Field.

Substitute:

H. W. CASE.

BASEBALL TEAM.

Schedule of Games Played during 1896-97.

FOOT BALL.

October 10,	Friends' School.
October 17,	Camp Street.
November 14.	Friends' School.
November 21,	Providence High School.

BASE BALL.

April 10, .	. Bulkley High School.
April 21,	Pawtucket High School.
April 24, .	. Brown Freshmen.
April 28,	. University Grammar.
May 1,	Friends' School.
May 8, .	English and Classical School.
May 22,	Providence High School.
May 29,	. Rogers High School.
June 5,	Friends' School.
June 12,	. East Greenwich.

Periodicals in Reading Room.

Congressional Record.

Science.

Rhode Island Pendulum.

Narragansett Times.

Sunday Telegram.

Washington Post.

Advocate of Peace.

Providence Journal.

New York Tribune.

Boston Herald.

Evening Call.

Congregationalist.

Pawtuxet Valley Gleaner.

Westerly Weekly.

Evening Telegram.

Forest and Stream.

Poultry Monthly.

Breeders Gazette.

Rural New Yorker.

Citizen.

The Farm Poultry.

Pomona Herald.

Successful Farmer.

National Geographic Magazine.

Art Amateur.

Illustrated London News.

Engineering Record.

Harper's Bazaar.

Forum.

Harper's Weekly.

Journal of School Geography.

Puck.

Monthly Bulletin.

The Rostrum.

Engineering Magazine.

Westerly Narragansett Weekly.

University Extension.

The School Review.

Quarterly Journal of Economics.

Westminster Review.

Quarterly Review.

The Electrical World.

Electrical Age.

Engineer.

Scientific American.

Power.

American Machinist.

Engineering.

Blacksmith and Wheelwright.

New England Journal of Education.

Journal of Military Service Institution.

Public Opinion.

Carpentry and Building.

Critic.

Nature.

Journal of United States Artillery.

Stillman's Journal.

Farmer's Voice.

Life.

Judge.

Farming.

Amer. Mathematical Monthly.

New England Magazine.

Educational Review.

Appleton's Popular Science Monthly.

Cosmopolitan.

Atlantic Monthly.

North American Review.

Chautauquan.

Scribner's.

American Naturalist.

Century.

Harper's.

Political Science Quarterly.

Journal of Society of Chemical Industry.

American Journal of Science.

The American University Magazine.

Journal of American Chemical Society.

Journal of Franklin Institute.

Popular Science Monthly.

Astrophysical Journal.

Journal of Geology.

Review of Reviews.

Agricultural Student.

" Eclectic."

IF it were not necessary to fill a page for the "Grist" we think it would not be worth while to begin a history of our society yet, we have done so little that merits commemoration.

The Eclectic was organized at Biscuit City, Oct., 1894, with a charter membership of thirteen. It was not formed for pleasure simply, but for literary and musical culture. Not long since an effort was made to give the society a purely social character; however it failed to receive the requisite assent of a majority of its members.

As we have no society room the meetings are held at the homes of the different members and occasionally in the chapel. Sometimes our gatherings are entirely of a social nature, and again interesting literary programmes are conducted by the members. Several evenings have been devoted to illustrated lectures given by members of the Faculty.

At intervals, varying in length, a paper, the Electic Herald, is edited by the members. This paper is quite popular among the students and a few of the articles which appear in "Grist" are taken from this famous literary production.

Officers.

W. J. TAYLOR, . . . President.
HARRIETTE F. TURNER, . . . Vice-President.
BESSIE B. HOXSIE, . Secretary and Treasurer.

Executive Committee.

W. J. TAYLOR, HARRIETTE F. TURNER, BESSIE B. HOXSIE, H. E. B. CASE, GRACE P. WELLS.

College Alumni Association.

———

GEORGE M. TUCKER,
PRESIDENT.

GEORGE A. RODMAN,
SECRETARY.

CHARLES L. SARGENT,
TREASURER.

Alumni, 1894.

	Course taken.	Occupation.	Address.
ADAMS, GEORGE E	Agr.	Assistant, R. I. Agricultural Experiment Station	Peace Dale, R. I.
AMMONDS, GEORGE C	Mech.	Mech. Dept., R. I. State Institutions, Corrections and Charities.	Howard, R. I.
ARNOLD, CHAPIN T	Agr.	Electrician	Providence, R. I.
BURLINGAME, GEORGE W.	Agr.	Teacher, Rockland, R. I.; Supt. Schools, Glocester, R. I.	Chepachet, R. I.
CLARK, HELEN M.		Student, Smith College	Kingston, R. I.
KNOWLES, JOHN F	Mech.	Instructor in Woodwork, R. I. College of Agr. and Mechanic Arts.	Kingston, R. I.
MADISON, WARREN B	Agr.	Landscape Gardener, Craig Colony.	Sonyea, N. Y.
MATHEWSON, ERNEST H.	Mech.	Teacher, Auburn High School	185 Williams St., Providence, R. I
PECKHAM, REUBEN W	Agr.	Student of Art.	Home address: Middletown, R. I. Oct. to April: 43 East 51st street, New York City.
RATHBUN, WILLIAM S	Agr.	Veterinarian	Wakefield, R. I.
RODMAN, GEORGE A	Mech.	Assistant, Bridge Dept., Worcester Div., N.Y., N.H. & H.R.R.Co.	Woonsocket, R. I.
SARGENT, CHARLES L	Agr.	Assistant Chemist, R. I. Agricultural Experiment Station	Peace Dale, R. I.
SLOCUM, SAMUEL W	Agr.	Carpenter	Westerly, R. I.
SPEARS, JOHN B.	Agr.	Farming	Foster Centre, R.I.
SWEET, STEPHEN A	Agr.	Farming	Slocumville, R. I.
TUCKER, GEORGE M.	Agr.	Student, University of Göttingen.	Unter Karspüle 14 Göttingen, Germany.
WILBUR, ROBERT A	Mech.	Farming	W. Kingston, R. I.

Alumni, 1895.

	Course taken.	Occupation.	Address.
ALBRO, LESTER F.	Agr.	Vocal Student—Jordan	185 Williams St., Providence, R. I.
BURDICK, HOWLAND	Agr.	Assistant Agriculturist	Kingston, R. I.
CLARKE, CHARLES S.	Mech.	Assistant Mechanic	Kingston, R. I.
ELDRED, MABEL D.	Mech.	Dr. Washburn's Private Secretary	Kingston, R. I.
HAMMOND, JOHN E.	Agr.	Assistant Agriculturist	Kingston, R. I.
OATLEY, LINCOLN N.	Mech.	Contractor,	Kingston, R. I.
SCOTT, ARTHUR C.	Mech.	Instructor in Physics.	Kingston, R. I.
TEFFT, JESSE C.	Mech.	Farmer and Miller	Jamestown, R. I.
WINSOR, BYRON E.	Mech.	Teacher	Summit, R. I.

Alumni, 1896.

	Course taken.	Occupation.	Address.
BROWN, MAY.	Mech.	Home.	Narragansett Pier.
GREENMAN, ADELAIDE M.	Mech.	Teacher	Kingston, R. I.
KENYON, ALBERT L.	Mech.	Silver Spring Bleachery	152 Smith Street, Providence, R. I.
MOORE, NATHAN L. C.	Agr.	Farmer.	Shannock, R. I.
TABOR, EDGAR F.	Mech.	Silver Spring Bleachery	152 Smith Street, Providence, R. I.
WILLIAMS, JAMES E.	Agr.	Farmer and Teacher	Summit, R. I.

Marriages.

Lincoln Nathan Oatley, '95, *to* Miss Mary Dyer Hull,

June 10, 1896,

AT TOWER HILL, R. I.

James Emerson Williams, '96, *to* Miss May Ursula Brown,

Sept. 1, 1896,

AT TOLLAND, CONN.

IN MEMORY

OF

ROBERT FRANKLIN TANNER,

Class of '96,

WHO DIED FEBRUARY 3, 1893.

IN MEMORY

OF

THOMAS COOK HAMMOND,

Class of 1900,

WHO DIED MARCH 14, 1897.

Biscuit City.

In a beautiful vale, in a quiet nook,
By a glassy pond and a babbling brook,
Lies a quaint little town, in its haunts so pretty,
This cute little village of " Biscuit City."

At the foot of the slope stood a woolen mill,
Many long years since has its wheel stood still ;
But now the bleaching walls remain
To tell how fire licked up the frame.

The old mill flume that has stood for years,
Has fallen from its stony piers ;
And back once more as all things must,
Change again to earthly dust.

The houses, which long have empty stood,
Are now the haunts of fairies good ;
And swallows in summer build their nests
On beam or rafter as they think best.

Above the mill in its fringe of trees,
With its twittering birds and humming bees,
The village lassie is very fond
Of her reflection in the pond.

And as you look at this peaceful scene,
On mossy bank of fringing green,
A frog sends forth his startling croak,
That lends to the air a mellow note.

A muskrat is swimming across the pond,
In search of the food he lives upon :
At the slightest sound of voice or bell
He is off like a flash in his watery dell.

The fishes, darting to and fro,
Breathe joy and gladness as they go ;
And then some fated, luckless fly,
For a fish's breakfast he must die.

Above on the slope for ages old,
Their roots entombed in leafy mould,
Stand grand old trees, their branches tossed,
Their trunks incased in feathery moss.

And at their foot lies a cocoanut cup,
Where a giant spring comes gurgling up ;
Whose waters have, for ages gone,
Sung in murmurs incessant song.

The joyful urchin from school let out,
Comes skipping along with gladsome shout,
And takes long drafts from this bountiful store
And capers away to school once more.

The student seeks this cool retreat,
From college boys and summer's heat ;
In this secluded spot to reach
For something books have failed to teach.

And the weary wand'rer, fraught with tares,
Forgets for once his worldly cares,
And wishes the brooklet's ceaseless song
Could to his soul this peace prolong.

Still the brook hurries on in careless dance
To join the pond's serene expanse :
Of all world's cares of pain and sorrows
The brook cares naught, it never borrows.

But issuing forth from the old mill race,
It leaves forever this enchanted place :
And chattering still, without one fear,
It is making harmony all the year.

Oh ! where will you find in books you've read,
Of charming things the poets said,
A happier spot in story or ditty,
Than the fairy-like place of " Biscuit City."   D.E.W.

An Episode.

When '98 was fresh.

An exciting class meeting was held in the recitation room in the Mechanical Building one day in April. It was called to discuss the practicability of planting a class tree; but the talk became confused and chaos reigned. A certain " Kid," well-known to the class, was one of the loquacious ones, who annoyed Mr. Harley's peace. At length Mr. Peckham remarked, " I move that we adjourn this meeting, never to meet again as Freshmen."

Mr. Harley rose in his ire, and, with a bow to Mr. Peckham, said, " I'll never meet you but when you're a Fresh-man." (*Repeated laughter*).

Mr. Peckham rose, bowed his thanks to Mr. Harley, and remained passably still thereafter.

Nonsense.

" *Good . . . . . morning . . . . . everybody!* "

First Sergt. T——r: " Right forward—fours left! March!"

Miss P——: " What is the color of Mongolians?" G——r: " They are negroes."

Dr. W—— : " What does $H Cl + Fe$ make!" D——y: "$H Cl Fe$."

E——y: " How many are there in the dancing class?" C——e: " Twenty fellows and four boys."

Dr. W—— (*explaining diagram*): " The H_2S, a colorless gas, is passing through this tube; you can see it running through."

Miss P——: " What happened when the Greeks met the Persians at Thermopylæ?" G——r: " They had a scrap.

Capt. C——e: " Count fours!" Private S——n: " 1, 2, 3, 4 !"

Motto of the third table in the Boarding Hall: " Wait—patiently wait."

Prof. S—— (*in physics*): " What is light?" Voice in rear: " Aluminum."

COMPANY A. THE FIRST DRILL.

Military Organization.

IN view of the great interest now taken in Military Drill in most educational institutions, a little about our military department will not seem amiss. The College is supported largely from the Morrill fund received from the United States government. This is appropriated on condition that military instruction be given to all able-bodied young men.

For the first four years of our existence there was no military department. But in the fall of 1894, Capt. Wotherspoon was detailed to the College, and the military department established. At first the cadets were organized into one company. This formation was maintained until last fall, when an increased number of students warranted the organization of a second company. We have in our equipment two three-inch rifles, and men are selected from the two companies of infantry for artillery duty. The non-commissioned officers and some of the privates also have a course in "wig-wag" signalling.

In the spring of 1896 we were invited to enter a squad against one from a local militia company in a competitive drill for a medal. We sent a squad, and the boys did splendidly, better even than we had hoped they would ; but our opponents were good, too. The judges had a hard problem before them to decide who won, but at last they did decide in favor of Co. F's squad. We had hoped that a similar contest might be arranged for this year, but unforeseen circumstances prevented it.

Last fall we took part in a parade in Wakefield, a G. A. R. celebration. Our battery furnished "music" before and after the parade, and with one company of infantry, joined in the column. We may say without conceit that the boys made a very good showing on this occasion.

And now a word for our military instructor. Capt. Wotherspoon is a most excellent officer, and a good disciplinarian. He has the respect of all and his work here has been most successful.

Military Companies.

Commandant.

W. W. WOTHERSPOON, Capt. Twelfth Infantry, U. S. A

Company A.

H. E. B. CASE,	Captain.
W. C. CLARKE,	Second Lieutenant.

Sergeants.

W. J. TAYLOR,	1st Sergeant.
W. F. HARLEY,	2d Sergeant.
S. W. WRIGHT,	3d Sergeant.
A. P. KENYON,	4th Sergeant.
A. F. GRINNELL,	5th Sergeant.

Corporals.

G. ROSE,	1st Corporal.
H. A. CONGDON,	2d Corporal.
B. E. KENYON,	3d Corporal.
H. W. ARNOLD,	4th Corporal.

Company B.

L. H. MARSLAND,	Captain.
A. A. TUCKER,	First Lieutenant.

Sergeants.

I. THOMAS,	1st Sergeant.
R. B. STROUT,	2d Sergeant.
M. A. LADD,	3d Sergeant.
W. S. CARMICHAEL,	4th Sergeant.
T. R. EDDY,	5th Sergeant.

Corporals.

C. F. KENYON,	1st Corporal.
W. L. W. CLARKE,	2d Corporal.
J. P. CASE,	3d Corporal.
A. W. BOSWORTH,	4th Corporal.

LIEUTENANT A. A. TUCKER,	Battalion Adjutant.
FIRST SERGEANT W. J. TAYLOR,	Sergeant Major.
H. W. CASE,	Bugler.

ARTILLERY DRILL

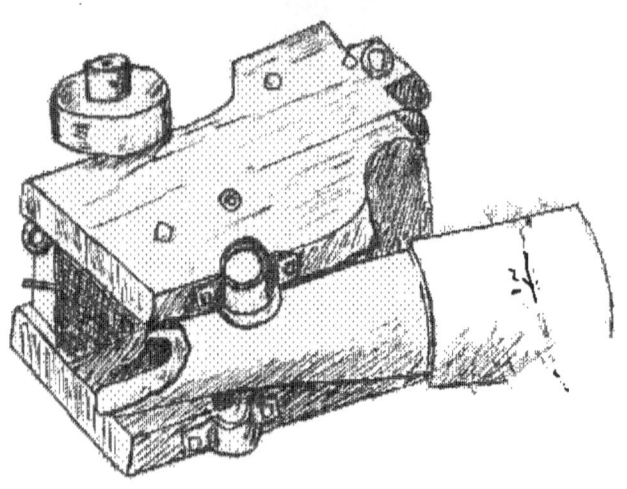

The Story of "Old Ben Butler."

THE remains of this old namesake, which has for the last few years been silently resting upon our front campus, has, I venture to say, a very unique history.

Born for the protection of our national unity, as the date (1861) upon its brazen sides may indicate, it served, we judge, faithful to its calling, upon one of our old warships throughout our late war. Several years after, the ship upon which it had given service, having passed its days of usefulness, was dismantled at Newport.

Just before an election in which Benjamin F. Butler was a prominent candidate, one of "South County's" well-known citizens, Captain George N. Kenyon, an ardent admirer of General Butler, purchased our friend in order to celebrate the General's election. This shows the origin of "Old Ben Butler's" name.

Now begins its peculiar career. To say the least, its new owner was a very odd person, and so some of the duties imposed upon "Old Ben Butler" were rather unusual. We hear stories that whiskey bottles were tightly corked and shot far out to sea; and Capt. Kenyon himself told me that at the end of a clam bake, held at his Gilbert Stuart home, the close of the feast was celebrated by filling "Old Ben Butler" with the remains of the clam chowder and other food and discharging it high into the air. So much for the history of "Ben Butler" previous to its connection with the school.

During the winter and spring of 1891-'92, the future of our beloved institution was a question of grave doubt. At one time its very existence seemed threatened. In the face of all discouragements, however, our cause was ably and vigorously championed by the principal, board of managers, and a few other firm friends. As the ripe fruits of this hard fought struggle, the existence of the institution was not only secured, but a very decided impetus forward was given, since the *school* was raised to the grade of a *college* with power to confer the degree, Bachelor of Science. It was for the purpose of sounding forth the loud acclamations of our joy for this victory that "Old Ben Butler" was brought here.

When in the spring it seemed likely that the legislature would pass the bill upon which our prosperity depended, the active desire for a jubilation seemed to fill the minds of all the students and certainly some of the faculty. A noise, and a big one, seemed to be the most natural way of expressing our feelings. Huzzahs, shot-guns, or the ringing of bells seemed far too tame. Nothing short of a cannon, and the largest one attainable—no mere toy—could begin to express the enthusiasm which possessed us. How to secure such a cannon was the next question. Kind and resourceful Mr. Rodman was, as usual, ready with a helping hand. He told of "Ben Butler" and the way to reach its owner. Our principal, soon to become our esteemed president, was consulted. He also was in sympathy with the scheme, and aided greatly by judicious counsel and financial assistance.

Accordingly Mr. Fred Prosens, an enthusiastic supporter of school spirit and a thoroughly good fellow, accompanied by your humble scribbler, set out upon the trip to see Capt. Kenyon and try to procure his cannon. The horse and carriage used on the trip were lent us by Prof. Towar, the nature of the errand no doubt increasing his willingness to do so. We saw Capt. Kenyon, who received us very cordially, and seemed heartily pleased with the idea of lending "Old Ben Butler" for our purpose. Joyfully we set out to find some one to move the cannon. Mr. Champlin, a neighbor of the Captain's, was soon secured, five dollars being his price for the job.

The cannon, smuggled in by a back way in order that the villagers might be the more thoroughly surprised at the demonstration, arrived at the school the very day the legislature passed our bill. Powder, which, by the way, was for blasting and not for cannon use, came from Westerly, and primers from Providence. Old stockings and other forms of underclothing were utilized in the making of the cartridges, all the students taking special pleasure in contributing to the supply.

All was in readiness when the news of success in the legislature came. Right heartily did "Old Ben" at once begin to thunder forth loud acclamations of triumph. Just as rapidly as the swab could be worked and a charge rammed home, the thunderings were repeated. By reason of active assistance in securing the cannon, friend "Pro" and myself were indulged in positions at the gun, numbers "one" and "two."

This vigorous demonstration lasted until nearly sunset, when it was deemed best to allow "Old Ben" to cool off a little and rest his hoarse throat. Not all of the students, however, were content to cease the celebration then. What a capital plan it would be to remind the villagers again at midnight that a new college had been created in the state! The two persons before-mentioned were the advisors and executors of this plan. The cartridges had been used up in the afternoon so that it was necessary to make others. At about half-past eleven, therefore, we quietly absented ourselves from the rest of the fellows and proceeded to what is now the blacksmith's shop, then in use as a pest hospital. We had been using two pounds of powder in a cartridge, but Capt. Kenyon had told us that "Ben" was easily good for four or five pounds. In order to prove the truth of his statement, of course it was necessary to use more than two pounds; accordingly we thought best to increase the size of the charge somewhat. The cartridge was made and "Old Ben" was once more called upon to proclaim the existence of our new college. Right vigorous was the response to our bidding. At previous discharges the gun had made no very forcible demonstration by way of motion, but this time accompanying the somewhat augmented thunder of the discharge, was a clean leap for joy of at least six or eight feet which landed the old fellow completely off the skids upon which it rested, careened considerably to one side. No damage was done, however, and after a deal of hard work with crowbars and so on, we managed to get the gun back once more to a position of stable equilibrium.

The idea of a sunrise gun formed the next link of our celebrating cerebration. Moreover, we had not quite reached the limit of charge which the Captain had assured us "Ben Butler" was amply able to handle. Another cartridge was made with a generous increase in the powder ration. At sunrise we were again tamping "Ben's" long stomach with a square meal containing a goodly supply of relishes and desserts in the shape of wet grass, sods, leaves, paper, etc. To be sure we thought that the meal would cause a considerable *strain* upon most stomachs, but we had great faith in "Old Ben's." To have him speak up loudly for "Old Kingston" was our desire. Alas! even so staunch a warrior as "Old Ben Butler" may at last be forced to succumb. The addition of the extra straw may indeed break the camel's back. The primer was snapped! one agonized leap into the air, a suppressed and "pumpkiny" moan of anguish, and "Old Ben Butler" fell back lifeless, dead of an over-*strained* stomach.

"Too bad" ventured one at last. Quietly we moved nearer where "Old Ben" lay. A few strokes of sympathy over his great broken body and we turned in silence toward the dormitory to spread the news of the sad calamity. Soon an atmosphere of sub-dued quiet pervaded the whole institution. "'Ben Butler' gone?" "Hard fate," was the response. Our president, always sympathetic and kind, was unusually quiet and full of feeling in his remarks in chapel that morning: sorrowful that "Old Ben Butler" was gone, but thankful that none of us were injured.

E. H. MATHEWSON, '94.

The

Third Annual Commencement

of the

Rhode Island College of Agriculture and Mechanic Arts,

Kingston.

June, - - - 1896.

———

COMMENCEMENT PROGRAMME.

SUNDAY, JUNE 21ST.

BACCALAUREATE SERMON,   4 P.M.
  by Rev. F. L. Goodspeed, of Springfield, Mass.

MONDAY, JUNE 22D.

RECEPTION BY THE BOARD OF MANAGERS AND FACULTY, 8 P.M.

TUESDAY, JUNE 23D.

GOVERNOR'S SALUTE, .   . 10.30 A.M.
REVIEW OF THE CADETS BY THE GOVERNOR, .   . 10.45 A.M.
COMMENCEMENT EXERCISES,   . 11.15 A.M.
RECEPTION AT THE STUDIO,   2 *until* 5 P.M.

COMMENCEMENT EXERCISES

In the Marquee.

PRAYER.

MUSIC.

THESIS, . THE WATER SUPPLY OF THE RHODE ISLAND COLLEGE.
Edgar Francis Tabor.

THESIS, ... CHARLES LAMB.
Mary Brown.

MUSIC.

THESIS, ... THE JACK-SCREW.
Albert Lewis Kenyon.

THESIS, ... FORESTRY OF RHODE ISLAND.
Nathan Lewis Cass Moore.

MUSIC.

GOVERNOR'S ADDRESS.

CONFERRING OF DEGREES.

PRESENTATION OF DIPLOMAS, *by* His Excellency Charles Warren
Lippitt, *Governor.*

BENEDICTION.

MUSIC.

Advertisements.

List of Advertisers.

Small service is true service while it lasts:
  Of our Advertisers, kind readers, scorn not one:
For the daisy, by the shadow which it casts,
  Protects the lingering dew-drop from the sun.

RHODE ISLAND COLLEGE

OF

Agriculture and Mechanic Arts.

TECHNICAL INSTRUCTION in agriculture, the mechanic arts, and the sciences. The four-year courses lead to the degree of Bachelor of Science, and after Seeptember, 1897, will be six in number: the course in agriculture, in mechanics, in chemistry, in physics and mathematics, in biology, and the general course. Special courses and a short course in agriculture and mechanics.

The courses offered to men are also open to women.

INSTRUCTION is given in

CHEMISTRY. Inorganic, organic, agricultural, physiological and sanitary, and the chemistry of the dyeing of textile fabrics. Laboratory practice, both qualitative and quantitative.

PHYSICS. Especial attention being given to electricity, and to photography and projection.

PHYSIOGRAPHY. With laboratory work and excursions.

AGRICULTURAL GEOLOGY. With especial relation to the formation of soils.

BOTANY. The later part of the course takes up the study of seed-plants of economic importance.

COMPARATIVE ANATOMY AND PHYSIOLOGY. Veterinary science, physiological psychology, civil government, political economy.

ZOOLOGY AND ANIMAL BIOLOGY.

AGRICULTURE. Theoretical and practical. Drainage, farm crops, stock-breeding, feeding of animals, fertilizers, dairying, apiary work.

HORTICULTURE. Olericulture, floriculture, pomology, vegetable pathology, horticultural literature, landscape gardening.

LANGUAGES AND HISTORY. English, comprising composition, rhetoric and literature; German—grammar, dictation, conversation, translation, reading; French; Latin; expression, including sight reading, extemporaneous speaking, recitations, and original orations; history, American, English, and general.

MATHEMATICS. Including civil engineering and astronomy.

MECHANICAL ENGINEERING. Strength of materials, mechanism, mechanics of engineering, steam engineering, metallurgy, mechanical drawing, wood-working, forging, iron work, pattern making, machine construction.

FREEHAND DRAWING AND MODELLING.

MILITARY DRILL AND TACTICS. Required of all male students. Infantry, artillery and signal drill; lectures on military science.

FACILITIES FOR INSTRUCTION

Include an excellent library, well equipped laboratories for chemistry, botany, mechanics and biology, the latter having a large collection of Rhode Island birds; and a farm embracing a large variety of soils for the departments of agriculture and horticulture. The location is especially advantageous for work in zoology.

ADMISSION TO ADVANCED STANDING is granted to candidates prepared for the work of any of the higher classes.

EXPENSES. Per year:—Room rent, $6; board, $108; fuel, $12; light, $3 to $9; books, $15 to $30; washing, $10 to $20; reading-room tax, $ .75; general expense, $1.50; laboratory fees, $6 to $30. Uniform, $15. Total for year,—minimum, $170; maximum, $250. Students of ability have opportunity to earn enough to pay a portion of their expenses.

EXPENSE FOR WOMEN. Board, including room rent, $3 per week; fuel and lights supplied at cost. Rooms furnished. Other expenses as above.

REQUIREMENTS FOR ADMISSION, 1897: Advanced arithmetic; geography; English grammar; United States History. No students admitted under fifteen years of age.

REQUIREMENTS FOR 1898: Arithmetic, algebra, plane geometry, English grammar, advanced English; United States history; geography, physiology; one year of German, French, or Latin.

A PREPARATORY DEPARTMENT will be opened in 1898.

Further details concerning the entrance requirements, with other information will be found in the catalogue, to be had on application to the President.

JOHN H. WASHBURN,

KINGSTON, R. I.

Because he goes to S. E. A.

Kenyon's  AT WAKEFIELD,

IS THE PLACE TO BUY YOUR

DRY ⸭ GOODS,

AND AT

THE BOSTON STORE,

AT NARRAGANSETT PIER.

ROBINSON'S

ESTABLISHED 1821.   WAKEFIELD, R. I.

Grocers.

Imported and Domestic Fancy Groceries, Table Delicacies.

OUR SPECIALTY:

TEA, COFFEE, FANCY CRACKERS,

Cigars and Tobacco. Pillsbury Flour. Ferris Hams and Bacon.

ELDRED BROS.,

DEALERS IN

High=Grade Groceries,  AND FRESH MEATS.

FRUITS, VEGETABLES, ETC.

95 Main Street. *Wakefield, R. I.*

Miss Leslie,

Fashionable ——

Dress Making.

Prices Reasonable.

Bank Building. Wakefield. R. I.

B. F. Brown & Son.

DEALERS IN

Beef, Pork, Mutton,

and

Poultry.

KINGSTON, R. I.

Why is the Junior Class noted for its Horticultural accomplishments?

Because it is the first to create an Annual.

(1.)

www.ingramcontent.com/pod-product-compliance
Lightning Source LLC
Chambersburg PA
CBHW020753020726
47495CB00008B/2416